· Kerstin Schoene ·

Monsters
aren't real...

To Wolf Erlbruch, to my family and to all
the nice people (and animals) who have
supported me in writing this book.

First American Edition 2012
Kane Miller, A Division of EDC Publishing

First published in Switzerland in 2011 by Bajazzo Verlag, Zürich,
as *Monster gibt es nicht...* by Kerstin Schoene.
This edition published under license by Bajazzo Verlag, Zürich.

For information contact:
Kane Miller, A Division of EDC Publishing
PO Box 470663
Tulsa, OK 74147-0663
www.kanemiller.com
www.edcpub.com

Library of Congress Control Number: 2011926825

Manufactured by Regent Publishing Services, Hong Kong
Printed March 2012 in ShenZhen, Guangdong, China

1 2 3 4 5 6 7 8 9 10
ISBN: 978-1-61067-073-9

· Kerstin Schoene ·

Monsters
aren't real...

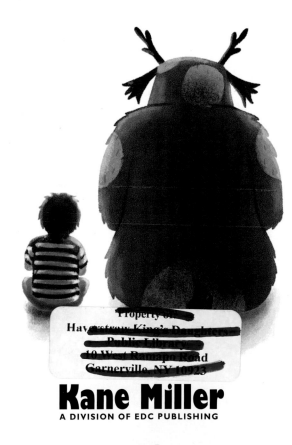

Kane Miller
A DIVISION OF EDC PUBLISHING

Monsters aren't real!

aren't real!

Monsters aren't real!

Monsters aren't real!

Monsters

aren't real!

Monsters aren't real!

Monsters

real!

Monsters aren't real!

Monsters aren't real!

aren't real!

Monster

What? No.

Monsters aren't real?
That can't be ...

That's not possible ...

Then what am I?

I'm as big as a monster.

I'm as strong as a monster.

I'm as scary as a monster!

Boo!!!

I'm a monster!

I'm a big, strong, scary monster,
and I'll prove it.

Monsters *are* real.

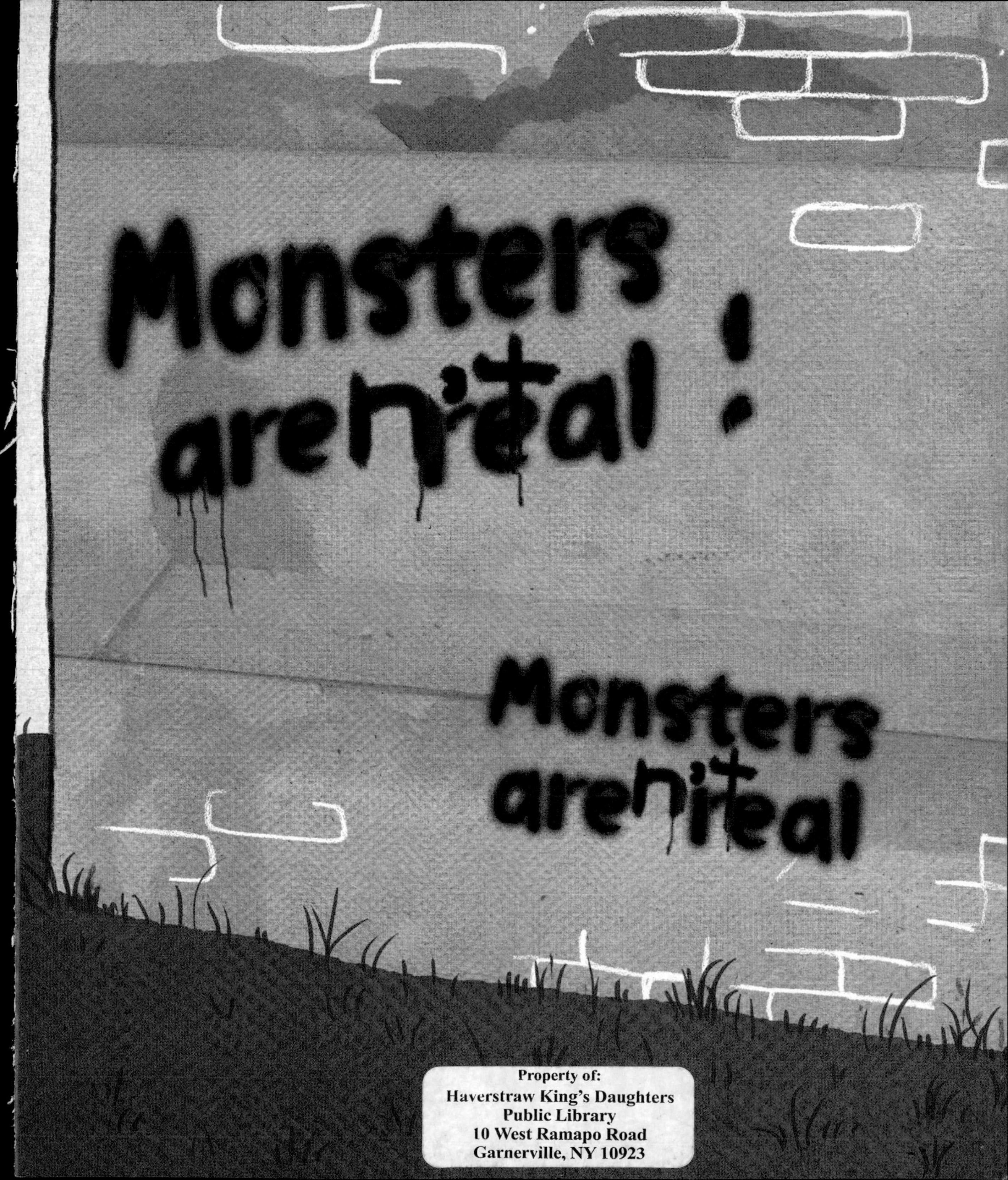
Monsters aren't real!
Monsters aren't real

That's it!
It's over!
I give up!

Monsters *aren't* real.

Monsters aren't real!
(sniff)
Monsters aren't real!
(sniff)
Monsters aren't real!
(sniff)

What? No!

Don't be silly.

We're two big, strong, scary
monsters, and we'll prove it.
Monsters *are* real.

Really.